SPACE EXPLORATION SUCCESSFUL FACTORS

JOHN LOK

Contents

Introduction
I write this book to aim to give my opinions to let readers to feel how operate or manage one space exploration organization in success.
I shall indicate these different factors which influence one successful space exploration successfully. Such as effective organization culture and communication factor, management team and strategy factor, space flight safe factor etc. It is suitable to any readers who pursue to know how manage or operate one space exploration organization in success.

Prologue

1

Space flight safe factor

To operate one space flight exploration organization, it needs to concern human safe flight factor. I shall indicate it needs to have these three stages to further develop its space exploration to continue to improve its safe space flight for every time of space flight.

Human future space flight missions will include these three stages to continue journey into space. The first stage is short term, NASA's return to flight after the Columbia accident. The second stage is mid term. What is needed to continue flying the shuttle fleet until a replacement means for human access to space and for other shuttle capabilities is available, and the third stage is long term, future directions for the kinds in space. Therefore, the space exploration organization can arrange the three stages to carry out any future space exploration activities. I believe it can improve every time of space flight more safe because it can ensure its space rocket engineering can be improved to raise safe level to let space people to catch to leave our Earth.

However, any human future space flight, which must be enhanced safety of flight when carry on any experimenting space flight exploration missions. Because NASA's safety performance is a very important factor to influence any space people confidence to catch every sky rocket to leave our Earth to do any space exploration activities. So, eliminating and catching rocket risks will be any beginning and end than during the middle of any space flight exploration journeys.

Space people's life is the most important assets of any space exploration journeys. Because of the dangers of ascent and re-entry, because of unknown space environment and because we are still relative new comers, operation of shuttle and indeed all human space flight must be viewed as a development activity.

Thus, any every time space flight exploration missions will need to encourage to invent new space transportation engines (machine) or fuel, e.g. nuclear fuel to reduce the any space exploration journey accident risks and achieves to spend the fastest time to arrive any new space exploration destination. Thus, I believe any new space exploration flight will improve the space transportation technology and invent more new fuel and new space rocket manufacturing materials for future human any unknown space exploration flight demand. The three stages of improving space transportation include as below:

The beginning stage, for example, the space shuttle is as somehow comparable to civil or military air transport. They are not comparable; the inherent risks of spaceflight are serious higher. The recognition of human spaceflight as a developmental activity requires a shift in focus from operations and meeting schedules to a concern for the risks involves. Thus, the space transportation tools will be improved to protect space passengers safety: the improving the ability to tolerate it, repairing the damage on a timely basis, reducing unforeseen events from the loss of crew and vehicle, exploring all options for survival, such as provisions for crew escape systems and safe havens , barring unwarranted departures from design standards and adjusting standards only under the most safety-driven process.

The mid-term stage, the present shuttle is not very safe to fly in space. Thus, focus on safe return to flight is very important to every space flight journey rules , they leave Earth and arrive any another new planet destination, then come back our Earth again in every space exploration journey (flight). Thus, the energy will be space transportation tool one important factor. If the space transportation tool has enough supply, which won't stay in space and can not fly in space suddenly. Thus, the every time of the human space flight will be taken more time and effort then would be reasonable to expect prior to return to flight. Thus, human space exploration organization needs have higher reliability organization structure to manage every space flight, e.g. one is separating technical authority from the function of managing schedules and cost. Another is an independent safety and mission assurance organization.

It is the capability for effective systems integration perhaps even more challenging than these organizational changes are the cultural changes requires. Thus, the cultural to safe and effective space rocket operations are real and substantial. If the space exploration organization has good culture to let every staffs can communicate easily. I believe the every time space exploration accident will be reduced. Examples include: the tendency to keep knowledge of problems contained within a center or program, technical decisions, without in -depth, peer-reviewed technical analysis, and an unofficial hierarchy or system created by placing excessive power in one office. Such factors interfere with open communication, the shared of lesson learned, cause duplication and expenditure of resources and create a burden for managers to reduce undesirable characteristics threaten safety.

Thus, any space exploration trip, rocket equipment safety and check are very important factor to prepare for every time space flight. The reason is that space flight must guarantee any space people who can come back Earth, if the rocket equipment are poor and lack maintenance. The, the space people whose life is dangerous. Due any space exploration organization mission require human presence in space. For example, president John Kennedy's 1961 charge to send Americans to the moon and return then safely to Earth. Thus, the space exploration organization has attempted to carry out a similar high priority mission that would justify the expenditure of resources on a scale equivalent to those allocated for project Apollo. Also, the space exploration organization has had to participate in the give and take of the normal political process in order to obtain the resources needed to carry out its programs.

Another main successful factor in the final stage, the space exploration organization needs have a clearly defined long term space mission to commit over the past decade to improve future space exploration flight safety by developing a second generation space transportation system. So, for long term, the space exploration organization should need to plan for future space transportation capabilities without making them dependent on technological breakthroughs.

For example, mission for a post Apollo effort that involved full development of low-Earth orbit, permanent outposts on the moon, and initial journeys to Mars planet. Since that rejection, these objective, have reappeared as central elements in many proposals, setting a long term vision for any space exploration flight programs in the future.

Thus, space organization future space exploration mission for 21 St century is to lead the exploration and development of the space frontier, advance science, technology and enterprise and building institutions and systems that make accessible vast new resources and support human settlements beyond Earth orbit from the highland of the Moon to the plains of Mars. Thus, the space exploration organization limit is to conduct the research required to plan missions to Mars and/or other distant destinations. This is the most safe space flight distance limit by the space rocket equipment, machine installation , quality and effort to guarantee space people life safety when who catch the space rocket life safety when who catch the rocket to leave Earth to arrive any space destination in any space flight. However, human travel to destinations beyond Earth orbit has not been adopted because it is too far space flight to cause accident risk. Hence, space exploration organization future invention of long term need is that the role of new space transportation capabilities in enabling whatever space goals need to choose to pursue for human present in Earth orbit vision.

In conclusion, space exploration organization needs to in-depth examination space shuttle safe issue, how to reach an inescapable design of the space shuttle, because that the design was based in many aspects on how absolute technologies and because the space shutter is now an aging system , but still developmental in character, it is in the space organization is interest to replace the shuttle as soon as possible as the primary aim for transporting humans to and from Earth orbit.

2

Space exploration organization mission and strategy

Space exploration organization communication strategy
I recommend any space exploration organization needs to the message concerns how the role of humans are actual physical presence in space exploration missions succeed. Because the positive message will give good idea of space exploration and then design and build means to carry out right space exploration direction to let humans to know whether any space exploration missions' goals, objectives and what humans benefits (welfares) who can earn.
The message includes such as these primary role of humans, therefore, is to provide the inspiration and create the vision which produces the motivation in those who then go on to make it a reality, e.g. the space exploration mission is to bring their human intellectual capability to bear in designing the technical systems required for space transportation and devising the scientific experiments

associated with space exploration from its beginnings.

Thus, any space exploration organization needs to let humans to know whether what benefits humans will earn after it carries out any space exploration experiments possibly. I believe that the exploration of the Earth's great expanse (the sea, the undersea world, air and land) is the ultimate role played by humans in body and in mind, and apply their intelligence, emotions and most importantly of all, their superior cognitive performance. So, this is the role now played by astronauts, explorers in the true sense of the world.

Why does space exploration organization need to be the role of communicator? The reason is because there is the role that space organization's need to play as communicators, journalists or other communication professional. It is they who provide the link between those involved in the project and taxpayer, who are entitled to be informed about the fascinating news on space.

Moreover, space exploration organization staffs need to give message to let humans to know why these playing roles are entirely human specific and can not be fulfilled by machines. For example, roles prior to human intervention, such as accompanying humans and performing tasks, which are repetitive and unpleasant out satellites too high a risk. By sending out satellites to explore our solar system humans have already begun to explore universe into reality Robots. On the other hand, may be things, but they are not visionaries and nor are they inventors or explorers. Any achievement they accomplish are in fact space organization staffs who designed and programmed them. Also, humans remain the best available cognitive machine in any environment that may be subject to significant variations relative to the model initially made of it. Thus, space exploration organization needs to explain, such as why in the general context of space exploration, even of most missions are robotic, remains technology challenges, it presents push engineers to the very limits of what can be achieved.

In the future, humans will earn these benefits or from any space explorations new invention possibly, such as fuel cells, the microcomputer, high performance materials, medical advances, new management techniques for major projects, quality and reliability control in industry etc.

The most important space exploration organization needs to positive message to let these groups of people to human what which is doing in our societies. Then, which will cause different actors to become involved from thinkers, visionaries and inspirational figures in the form of writers and film makers to scientists, engineers, philosophers, politicians, economists, physicians, journalists, authors, space travelers (astronauts), but also adults and children space story book readers alike. Thus, space exploration organization is truly multi disciplinary enterprise. Moreover, in the present day, normal escapes being concerned by space, as much due to its contribution to daily life and the knowledge it beings of the Solar system and the universe. It seems space exploration organization will influence human past history will be changed to develop. Whether it brings positive or negative change. The space organization must have responsibility to keep its any space exploration missions leader position in our Earth. It implies it is also one social responsible organization for future global human benefit (welfare).

Also space exploration organization needs to let humans know what it's future aims (intentions) are to let humans know whether why it plan to implement. Such as it needs to choose destination has typically been the Moon, it had increasingly come to focus its attention on Mars and even further afraid. Moreover, it also needs to know humans to know the modes of future space transportation which described have tended to be those of the period concerned: ships, horses, birds, balloons, canons, rockets and even others of a more esoteric nature, even solar sail or nuclear soil further space transportation technology development. In addition, space exploration organization can need to describe where are further orbital space stations in space different locations and explained the various applications of satellites and spacecrafts to let human to know clearly.

Even, space exploration organization also need to let humans to know what are their technical challenges, it will encounter in any space exploration stages to let humans to know. Although, the complexity and changer involved in spaceflight is such for a long time to come there will be a need for experts, whose focus by necessity. So, the general public will know or recognize why it's technical challenges will cause and how it will attempt to solve these technical challenges. It aims to let humans to ensure more than 40 years of spaceflight, the adventive of space, which for technical reasons is inevitably reserved to a " happy few", remains very much the preserve of specialists, cooperation to research how to solve any technical challenges to achieve success in any space exploration mission consequently.

Space exploration organization team leaders and their teams

The first team members are program chiefs and mission message are request to the be backroom generals with a great many human qualities. They must having to achieve great technical exploits and manage their teams with care when at the same time ensuring they deliver in timing and one budget. Even the very best robot-machines and computers available are of no help to them in coming up with the initial idea and architecture for their systems. Indeed, in that initial stages, some program chiefs, even insist on their management team using only paper and pencil writing. Once the concept has been defined, they then need computers to speed up and develop the project.

When these leader figures are fortunate enough to see their program in orbit and crowned with success, their experience and methods can be of use, to equally computer technical sectors. They can also be passed on to following generations, thus safeguarding, for reasons of economics and security, the know how acquired by their teams. Another team members are scientists and those responsible for the technical side of program are not generally skilled communicators by nature, those with communication to public , such " communicators" could be awarded special prizes. Communication on the space sector can't be left to " communication specialists". Otherwise, there is a risk, it will be perceived to be doomed to failure.

Space exploration organization education is such as strategy space exploration organization communicator, are there to inform, the teaching profession for its part, must perform a vital education role, helping people understand the universe in which they live. Space exploration represents a unique opportunity to explain the situation of our planet within the solar system, asking questions such as: How does the sun function? What are the origins of the Moon? Why does Venus have such a pronounced greenhouse effect? Is there or has there ever been life on Mars? Do asteroids pose a serious threat? There are all questions which today, our schools don't even attempt to answer. Thus, space exploration organization can be one educator role, instead of space explorer role.

Thus, space exploration organization has mission to assist universities to promote space exploration education knowledges. It brings this question: What other technological and scientific program is better equipped to meet these objective than space exploration , with its crewed emissions component. So crucial to the promotion of a European industry, so visible to the general public and so efficient in inducing younger generations to take up scientific and technical careers? Thus, the space education courses can include space exploration industrial applications, a new area of investigation to scientific fields, fundamental physics, cellular and vegetal biomedical research and human and animal physiological research etc. subjects. For example, teaching how to go to Mars or other planets and manage to live these will require a knowledge of how to energy in innovative ways for the purposes of managing electricity generation requirement will be to learn how to manage scare resources in an efficient way (air, water and waste recycling). So, teaching of progress will have to be made in advanced robotics in particular in the area of effective and human robot interaction.

In conclusion, all these space exploration science education knowledge will be important to be taught to let younger to pursue space resource exploration dream for human future live

3

Space exploration organization's Human space life science factor

What is human space life science strategy?

One space exploration organization needs have good human resource strategy to implement every space exploration mission. Critical to this expansion of human presence in space science will enable mission success by focusing on risk reduction and optimizing astronaut health an productivity through space organization's human-centered science, operations and engineering core capabilities.

Thus, the space life science strategy's strategical goals, and objectives were developed on the basis of a situational analysis conducted by key members of the space life science civil service and contractor
community, and are consistent with agency goals and scenarios for the future.
This strategy mission is to optimize human health and productivity for space exploration and its vision is to

become the recognized world leader in human health, performance and productivity for space exploration . It's strategic goal are aimed at driving innovations in health and human system integration, adapting its portfolio and strategies to the changing environment and creating enthusiasm for space exploration through education. Also, the space life sciences human strategy aims to achieve every space exploration research more success, more efficient, focuses on client (human) needs and facilities communication of risk to public and the value of space life sciences to its stakeholders (governments, universities, societies).

How can human space life science strategy implement?

The space exploration organization needs to be dependent upon healthy, productive astronauts to achieve mission success. Thus, space people health are very important factor to influence their every time space flight in success. If the space people have unhealthy bodies , which will influence whose work performance and every time space exploration mission can't finish easily. Thus, the human space life science strategy needs to ensure every space person has health body to work efficiently and reduce whose death or accident risk when they are working in space environment, due to space environment is one strange bad color environment and it is very difference to our Earth environment to unsafe to work by these factors:

such as, it's temperature is low, cold and no air or oxygen to be supplied to let human to breathe and it has unknown diseases in space. Thus, they will face any life danger when are working in space environment. If space organization lacks one human space life science strategy to help them to fight any unknown attack from space environment. The, they are very dangerous to attempt to catch space rockets to leave our Earth to do any space exploration activities.

However, the space life science strategy can divide these three timeframes consistent with

- Near –term (1-5 years)
- Mid-term (6-10 years)
- Long-term (11-20 years)

The space life science strategy mission is that optimize human health and productivity for space exploration . Thus, all space life sciences human health and countermeasures research, medical operations, habitability and environmental factors activities, and directorate support functions are ultimately aimed at achieving this mission. Their activities enable mission success, optimizing human health and productivity in space before, during and after the actual space flight experience of their flight crews, and include support for ground-based functions.

The space life science strategy vision is to become the recognized world leader in human health, performance and productivity for space exploration. Thus, to achieve the vision for space exploration , they must drive human health, performance and productivity innovations, adapting

their strategy to the changing environment. To do this, the space exploration organization needs have a future scenario for space life science strategy such as below:

- Future core capabilities will include the expertise to address space medicine, the physiological and behavioral effects of space flight, space environment definition and space human factors.

- Research plans are on the basis of a standard –based risk mitigation approach to ensure goals are achieved.

● Civil servants will balance delivery of health and performance services and focused research and technology development with smart buyer and management expertise to integrate space life sciences efforts.

● Strategy relationships will be utilized to achieve the full complement of space life sciences core

capabilities necessary to achieve vision and enable mission success.

● Space life science strategy will transition from being a managing partner to a contributing partner, arranging the resources and innovations of other organizations to meet specific exploration needs, e.g. universities, government or business biomedicine organizations.

● Operations will effectively transition the space people skills and facilities from shuttle and assess and engage in additional government and commercial space flight operations opportunities where appropriate.

● An expanded client base that may include additional international and academic partners , as well as commercial alliances.

Situation analysis

A situation analysis was conducted to determine its mission and to identify the factors most likely to influence its strategy development and affect achievement of its goals and objectives . It will trend to concern life sciences and space flight of internal and external environments. It needs to image these assumptions to decide its situation analysis as below:

Thus, the first assumption is that it needs to assume that human will continue to be an important component of the vision for space exploration, and as a result there will be an ongoing need for space life sciences core capabilities, including human-centered science, operations and engineering to mitigate the health and performance risk of human space flight.

Another assumption is in the longer term, there will be a greater focus on crew autonomy and increased human-robotics interaction as mission durations increase and are extended to travel to and on planets, and as a result, these is a continued need for research and development activity focused need for research and development activity focused on exploration risk reduction.

The next assumption is the pace of biomedical change will continue to be more rapid in external versus internal environments. Thus, solutions are more kinds of likely to be developed external to fight any different new unknown new diseases to attack to influence space people health to be poor , even cause death in possible.

What are space life science strategy goals?

On health innovation hands, the space exploration organization will drive advances in medical and environmental health for space flight in order to meet established space life standard and mission needs. Thus , innovation on medicine and biomedical / environment technology and processes will be developed, implement and incorporated into mission achievement.

On education hand, it needs to train in multidisciplinary life sciences, experts in exploration life science and that this is a continuous infusion of space ,life science into the public , government , academic and commercial sectors. Thus, the space life science education aim includes to teach the human system risk management, strategic relationship of any space missions, future space business model and space communication strategies.

The goal-specific strategies and measurable objectives can be developed for years 1 to 5 years It's objectives can include: optimize internal core capabilities throughout the planning cycle to enable the vision for space exploration with budgetary constraints, establish strategic relationship to achieve the full complement of life sciences capabilities necessary to be best in class , establish a center to integrate human health and performance efforts and expertise for space exploration worldwide, implement an internal and external communication plan to increase the life sciences value to encourage space human life education development for long term in commercial space flight sector.

Health innovation goal

Thus, one space exploration organization whose health innovation strategy is the main factor to influence its any overall space exploration missions inn success. Thus, it must need to spend more money and time and resource to ensure its health innovation implement can be succeed to reduce further every time space people's mission of physical illness or death or accident which are caused by space diseases . Thus, it will drive advances in medical and environmental health for space flight in order to meet establish space flight health standards and mission needs. Also, it needs to attempt to do any biomedical experiments to avoid space people who can contact to cause illness from any undiscovered space diseases.

Hence, the invention of space medicine, biomedical / space environmental technology and processes will be developed, implemented often every day/ IT needs to seek or gather every time practical space environment biomedical existing data and knowledge as a base for launching health technologies and to revise every time space biomedical experiment failure to find failure reasons to achieve the most absolute discovered any space unknown diseases biomedical experiment results. Thus, the improved methods and practice or recording data must concern to goals for human space exploration, attempting towards data gathering top continuing to achieve the best levels of evidence for answering operational and clinical questions regarding human health, safety and performance, during space flight and exploration and an evidence-based risk management approach to prioritize tasks.

The space biomedical experiments data gathering can consider human factors engineering, habitability design and human-robotics interaction will be recorded to analyze experiment result every time. These results will be developed, implemented and incorporated into mission architecture solutions to address the human as an element of the overall space system.

Prediction on future trends in human space flight and future space human life science strategy relationship.

In the future, the relationship between future trends in human space flight and future space human life science will be more close. These reasons are that the trends in terrestrial life sciences will save as change drivers for space life sciences, include advanced in nano health, genetics, biocybernetics, self-constructing materials, human computer interfaces, medical and pharmaco-therapeutics, multi-scale physiological modelling and other biomedical technologies.

In conclusion, due to space exploration organization's objective is low tolerance for a risk and emphasis on risk quantification and reduction activities. Thus, the space human life science
strategy will be one important factors to cause any one space exploration organization's any missions in success.

Why does Japan space organization consider space human life science?

Japan has acquired and advanced various space technologies. Through, these technologies level to allow to play a core role in the international human space activities . However, it's space exploration success is due to it concerns to achieve its space human life science strategy for its main point.

What social benefit from its utilization of the space environment to Japan. Because it concerns how to protect space human life during who are working in space. Thus, it can bring more social benefits to develop its space exploration industry for long term as below:

● Because it's space people can have health bodied, so who can attempt to any space science exploration experiments in space
environment as well as space human life science can raise Japan space people confidence to attempt to do every time. space exploration activities in space environment. Consequently, they have confidence to catch rockets to go to space to gather various resource to do any space exploration to get research results more easily, which were achieved through utilization , such as micro gravity environment, that could not be produced on the ground, these outcomes include: protein crystal growth, that may

lead to the development of new drugs, materials creation for next-generation semi-conductors, and establishment of the technology for cubesats deployment, etc.

● Due to Japan space exploration organization concerns space people health issue. Thus, it has manned space flight capability can conduct youth development activities , with their own astronauts and such astronaut-led activities have aroused the younger generation's interest in outer space, taught them the importance of making efforts to making of one health space scientists confidence to pursue this space exploration industry.

Hence, when all Japan space scientists who own health bodies, then who can be one expansion of humankind's space of activities in this area create knowledge of planetary science and the quest of health space life and also contributes to the increase and accumulation of intellectual assets of all human beings.

The most reason of Japan's belief of space human life science strategy is very important , because it needs to prove human can live in space environment. Thus, if Japan's space scientists can have health bodies to do any space exploration experiments, then who is still health to go back Earth. Then , it proves the life support technologies , the space environment and health management and the maximum energy conservation. This leads to the enhancement of corporate brands and international appeal of technical capabilities , and is directly linked to resulting problems Japan faces , such as its aging population and lack of natural resources.

In conclusion, space human life science will influence Japan space exploration industry more success. Otherwise, if it chooses not to implement this space human life strategy. It won't have enough health space scientists to attempt to catch rockets to go to space to do any space exploration experiments more success in long term, e.g. seeking Earth another planets to provide Japan people to live, raising Japan young space scientists confidence to attempt to go to space to do any experiments because the Japan space exploration organization can provide new bio medical invention to supply when they are catching in the space rockets. If they feel that they are comfortable, they can eat or drink the new bio medical invention to avoid the space disease attack to cause their death or physical illness threat.

In conclusion, space human life science is very important factor to influence future every time human space exploration mission successfully.

www.ingramcontent.com/pod-product-compliance
Lightning Source LLC
Chambersburg PA
CBHW020947160726
47993CB00007B/2977